MW01137112

Petunia

the ugly pug

Heather Grovet

Pacific Press® Publishing Association
Nampa, Idaho
Oshawa, Ontario, Canada
www.pacificpress.com

Edited by Bonnie Tyson-Flyn
Designed by Dennis Ferree
Cover and Inside art by Mary Rumford

Copyright © 2002 by
Pacific Press® Publishing Association
Printed in the United States of America
All Rights Reserved

Additional copies of this book may be purchased at
http://www.adventistbookcenter.com

Library of Congress Cataloging-in-Publication Data

Grovet, Heather, 1963-
    Petunia the ugly pug / Heather Grovet
        p. cm. — (Julius and friends; 7)
    Summary: Nine-year-old Kyla adds patience,
prayer, and training to the love she has for her pet pug
Petunia so that she will become the dog she has
always wanted.
        ISBN 0-8163-1871-9
        [1. Pug. 2. Dogs. 3. Dogs—Training. 4. Christian life.]
I. Title II. Series.
        PZ7.G931825 Pe 2002
        —dc21   2001036713

02 03 04 05 06 • 5 4 3 2 1

Contents

Other Books in the Julius and Friends Series

Dedication

To Mom and Dad,
who taught me to love books—and to love
animals!

CHAPTER

1

The Perfect Dog?

Nine-year-old Kyla Hanton jumped up on the doorstep and ran her fingers through her short brown hair. Normally Kyla didn't care how she looked, but this was an important day!

Kyla's mother stepped up beside her and smiled. "You look fine," she said.

"Good," Kyla said. She reached out one finger and pushed the doorbell. "I want to look nice for my pug," she told her mother and older brother, Jason, "because my dog is going to be wonderful."

Jason rolled his eyes.

"My dog," Kyla continued, "is going to be beautiful."

"It'll probably look better than you do!" Jason teased, tugging on a strand of Kyla's hair.

"My dog," Kyla said, ignoring her brother, "is going to be smart."

"I'm coming," a voice called from inside the house. A dog began to bark loudly in the background.

Kyla squirmed impatiently and glanced at the sign by the door. The paint was peeling, and the sign was crooked, but Kyla could still make out the words—Rosewood Kennels.

"My dog—" Kyla began.

There was a thump, and then the door swung open.

Just inside the door stood an elderly woman wearing a faded yellow dress. Her hair was gray, and bits of it stood on end as though she had just gotten out of bed a few moments before. But Kyla wasn't interested in the woman—all she wanted to see was the small black dog that the woman held in her arms.

"My dog—" Kyla said eagerly, reaching out to touch and pet and hold it.

But then she stopped and looked at the dog again.

Something was wrong. Surely this wasn't

the wonderful, beautiful, smart pug that Kyla had come all these miles for. There must be some terrible mistake!

"Come in, come in!" the woman said, waving at them with her free hand.

"My dog?" Kyla asked, her eyes darting back and forth.

"Your dog!" Jason hissed in her ear. "Your dog is UGLY!"

The Hanton family filed into the house.

"Welcome," the woman said, smiling sweetly. "Welcome to Rosewood Kennels. Mind you, we're really not a kennel anymore. All my babies are gone, except for this one. Here, have a seat, Dearie. And here's a chair for you, Young Man. You must be tired after your long drive here today."

Mrs. Hanton nodded her head but didn't say anything.

The woman then realized that everyone was staring at the dog.

"Oh, my," the woman said. "Here you've come all this distance, and I haven't shown you your baby yet. This," she said, shifting the dog to her other arm, "is Petunia."

Mrs. Hanton nodded again and cleared her throat.

Kyla looked around the room quickly. Maybe this was a mistake. Maybe there was another black pug in the room, another dog that was as wonderful and beautiful and smart as she had been expecting. Any other dog would be fine, just not the one that lay limply in the woman's hands.

"And I understand that Petunia is going to be all yours, Young Lady," the woman said. "Aren't you a lucky girl—a doggy of your very own!"

The woman held the dog out toward Kyla. Kyla just stared at it.

One of Mr. Hanton's friends had a pug puppy, so Kyla knew what to expect. She knew that pugs had funny flat faces and wrinkled foreheads and tight curly tails. But there was something wrong with this pug. Its flat face was covered with brown scabs. Sticky green drainage crusted around its eyes. One ear was hairless and flopped listlessly. The dog was so skinny that its ribs showed, and there was a large bald spot on its neck. No, this was not a normal pug.

Kyla turned from the dog and looked at her mother. Mrs. Hanton's face was covered by an enormous frown, and her eyebrows were raised.

"She's such a darling little thing, aren't you, Petunia Baby?" the woman cooed. "But she's been so sad since her puppies died. She needs someone to take good care of her, don't you, Petunia Baby?"

The lady thrust the dog into Kyla's hands and took a step backward.

"What stinks?" Jason muttered, backing up a step.

Kyla knew what smelled so terrible. It was the dog. The smell now was overpowering—not just a normal wet-doggy smell but the smell of garbage or rotten fruit.

Poor thing! Kyla thought in horror. *But I'd never want a pet like this. I want a perfect dog.*

The black dog had been lying without movement in Kyla's arms. But now she raised her face to look at Kyla.

Two bright brown eyes fastened firmly on Kyla. The dog studied her carefully, and then slowly the small tail began to wag.

Kyla couldn't look away from the dog's eyes. They seemed to speak to her. *Help me,* they said. *Care for me. Love me.* The tail began to wag faster—and then faster again.

Kyla reached down one finger and gingerly touched the dog.

Petunia licked Kyla's hand and then snuggled close into her arms. Petunia's tail continued to thump happily.

Suddenly Kyla didn't care if the dog was ugly or skinny or smelled bad. She knew this dog needed her.

Mrs. Hanton was talking quietly to the woman. "I don't think we're interested," her mother said.

Kyla touched her mom's shoulder. "I want her," Kyla said.

Jason hooted in the background.

"Pardon me?" Mrs. Hanton asked. Her eyebrows shot even higher.

"I want her," Kyla said, firmer this time.

"Of course you do, Dearie," the woman said. She fussed around, gathering a faded pink leash and a frayed collar. "I have all of her things packed. Here's her bowl and her blanket, and here's a book I have on pugs. I won't be needing it anymore, and I thought maybe you'd like it."

"You want this dog?" Mrs. Hanton asked in a tight voice.

"I want her," Kyla said. "And she wants me."

The lady passed the blanket and leash to Jason, who held them at arm's length. "I'm so glad my darling is going to a good home," the woman bubbled. "She's such a dear doggy. But my son doesn't think I should be living alone anymore, and they won't let me keep a pet in the retirement home."

"I'll take good care of her," Kyla promised. The dog wagged its tail again when it heard Kyla's voice.

Mrs. Hanton slowly pulled out her checkbook.

"That will be one hundred dollars," the woman said. "A very good deal, I can tell you. You won't find a dog like this just anywhere."

"I hope not!" Jason whispered. Kyla glared at him, but the dog's tail continued to wag gently.

The family was halfway down the sidewalk when the woman called from the doorsteps.

"Come back, Dearie," she said.

Kyla tightened her grip. She wasn't going to let Petunia return to that house, no matter what the woman wanted.

But the woman wasn't calling for Petunia. Instead, she waved a piece of paper in the air. "Don't forget your baby's registration papers," the woman called. "Her real name is Black Petunia Lass."

CHAPTER

2

Bitten in the Car

"You're not actually taking that thing home, are you?" Jason asked as the family climbed into the car.

Kyla ignored him and settled the small black dog on her lap before fastening her seatbelt.

"That dog's sick," Jason said. He unrolled his car window. "And I'm going to be sick, too, if I have to smell that thing all the way home!" He pinched his nose and made a face at Kyla.

"Stop picking on my dog," Kyla said loudly. "There's nothing wrong with her."

"That's not correct, Kyla," Mrs. Hanton said. "That dog is sick." She glanced back at Kyla and then hesitated.

"What do you mean?" Kyla asked. She carefully ran her hand down the dog's back. Petunia looked up into Kyla's face and wagged her tail again.

"Honey," Mrs. Hanton's voice was soft and kind now. "I'm really worried about that dog. It's very, very sick. I hope Dr. Marsh will be able to help it."

"Her name's Petunia," Kyla said quickly. "And she's just skinny."

"No, Kyla," Mrs. Hanton said. "That dog isn't just skinny. She's sick. That's why I didn't want to buy her."

Kyla felt her eyes begin to fill with tears. She blinked hard, trying to hold them back. "We couldn't just leave her there, could we?" Kyla asked. "She could die there."

"Yes, Honey," Mrs. Hanton said. "She could die there. But what if we can't help her either?"

"What should we do?" Kyla asked. This time a tear spilled down her cheek and landed on the dog's back.

Jason looked at her and shook his head. But he didn't say anything as he passed Kyla a tissue.

"The very first thing we do," Mrs. Hanton said, "is stop at Dr. Marsh's veterinary office. He'll tell us what to do."

Kyla looked out the car window and sniffed. It just wasn't fair! Her parents had promised her a dog when she turned nine. Kyla had spent months dreaming about the perfect dog—wonderful and beautiful and smart.

When Kyla's dad had invited his friends and their new pug puppy over a few months before, Kyla had fallen in love with their puppy instantly. Their pug, whose name was Winky, was perfect. He was cuddly and cute and friendly. Kyla couldn't help compare the two dogs in her mind. First there was Winky, with his funny little wrinkled face and round body. And then there was Kyla's new dog, Petunia, who was so sick and ugly that no one wanted her.

She can't die, Kyla thought sadly. *I love her already.*

The drive home seemed to take even longer than normal. Mrs. Hanton listened to her favorite gospel music tape and hummed slightly off-key to herself. Jason fell asleep with his head against the car window. All Kyla could do was sit and look at Petunia. And the more she looked, the more she worried.

Dear God, Kyla prayed in her mind, *please help Petunia get better. I can tell she's going to be a good dog; she just needs our help. Please don't let her die. Amen.*

Petunia seemed to be happy enough riding in the car. She snuggled her head down into Kyla's lap, wagged her tail a few times, and then fell asleep.

"You're a good dog, aren't you?" Kyla whispered to Petunia. "Except for the smell." The whole car now smelled like a garbage truck. "Tonight you get a bath," Kyla said.

They were almost home when Kyla's stomach began to itch. She scratched, but the itch didn't go away. In a few moments there was another itchy spot, this time on her left side. And soon there were two more itchy spots on her back. Kyla shifted the dog from one arm to the other and scratched all the itchy spots. She wiggled and scratched and wiggled some more.

Finally Jason stretched and yawned and opened his eyes. "Would you sit still?" he grumbled.

Kyla rubbed her shoulder and then her forehead. "I can't help it," Kyla said. "Something's biting me."

"Aw, you're just imagining things," Jason said with a yawn. Suddenly he reached around and swatted at his own back. "Hey," he said. "Something just bit me."

By now Kyla was so itchy she could hardly stand it. She carefully set the black dog down on the seat beside her, and using both hands, began to scratch herself frantically. That itch! It felt as if something were crawling around inside her shirt, biting in a dozen different places!

Jason slapped at his back several times and then began to paw at the front of his shirt. "Mosquitoes," he said. He ruffled the hair up on the back of his head and suddenly his eyes got enormous. "It's not mosquitoes," he said loudly. "It's fleas! That crazy dog has fleas!"

"Petunia doesn't have fleas," Kyla said weakly. But even as she spoke she saw something tiny and dark jump onto her shirt. Kyla bent over and looked at the tiny thing. Why, it had legs! It was a bug!

"Fleas!" Kyla shrieked. The bug jumped off her shirt and disappeared from sight.

"Get them off me!" Jason yelled.

"Are you sure you saw a flea?" Mrs. Hanton asked.

"I saw it!" Kyla yelled.

Mrs. Hanton frowned. "Well, we'll be at the veterinary clinic soon," she said. "I'm sure you'll both survive until then."

But by the time they pulled up at the

clinic, Mrs. Hanton was also scratching wildly.

The three of them shot out of the car as soon as it stopped. Jason pulled off his shirt and shook it frantically. Kyla would have laughed at her mother, who was hopping around shaking her legs, if she hadn't been too busy scratching herself. Kyla wished she could yank her shirt off too, but that would have been much too embarrassing—even if it did feel as if a thousand fleas were dancing under her shirt.

No one was watching as the small black dog got to her feet and walked to the edge of the car seat. No one was watching as the small dog looked around curiously and then jumped awkwardly from seat to car floor to gravel parking lot. And no one was watching as the dog sniffed around a few times and then ambled off across the parking lot and into the tall grass and clover in a nearby hay field. In a few moments the little dog was out of sight—and no one in the Hanton family had noticed a thing.

CHAPTER

3

Disappearing Dog

It was Jason who first noticed the open car door. "Hey, Dog-Woman," he called to Kyla, "you had better get your pet before her fleas get away."

Kyla scratched one more time and then hurried over to the open door. "Poor Petunia," she cooed. "I forgot all about you, didn't I? Come on, Baby, we're going to go see the doctor."

But there was no sight of Petunia. Kyla looked in the back of the car and then the front of the car and then under the car. Where could Petunia have gone?

"Petunia!" Kyla called loudly. She looked around the parking lot.

A dirty blue half-ton truck and horse trailer stood beside the vet clinic. As Kyla watched, a man in a cowboy hat came out of the clinic and climbed into the truck. It started with a loud roar and began to roll slowly forward.

"Petunia!" Kyla screamed. She ran wildly toward the truck, waving her hands. What if Petunia were hiding under the truck! She would be run over! "Petunia!" Kyla screamed again.

The cowboy didn't notice a thing. In a moment the truck and trailer were out of sight.

"What's your problem?" Jason asked, staring as Kyla raced over to the place where the truck had been parked.

"What if Petunia was run over?" Kyla panted.

But there was no sign of the dog

"Petunia!" Kyla called again.

Now they all began to search for Petunia. They checked the parking lot, then behind the veterinary clinic, and then around the nearest buildings. But there was no sign of the small black dog.

"Where could she be?" Kyla asked. She was nearly in tears again.

"I really don't know," Mrs. Hanton said. She stopped and scratched her leg, thinking.

"But don't worry; someone will find her."

"But she's sick," Kyla wailed.

"Was her name on the dog collar?" Jason asked.

"She didn't have her collar on yet," Kyla said. "I thought it would rub her sore neck."

Mrs. Hanton sighed. She looked worried but didn't seem to know what to do.

"I want my dog back," Kyla said.

"Look, everyone," Mrs. Hanton suddenly said. "We haven't done something important yet. We haven't prayed for God's help."

"Oh, Mother," Jason groaned.

"Don't you think God can help us?" Mrs. Hanton asked, shooting a look at Jason.

The boy quickly nodded his head. "Oh, I know He can," Jason said. "But we'll look like real idiots standing out here praying. Everyone can see us."

"There's nothing foolish about prayer and trusting in God," Mrs. Hanton said. She took Kyla's and Jason's hands.

"May I pray?" Kyla asked. "After all, Petunia is my dog."

"Go ahead," Mrs. Hanton said.

Kyla closed her eyes. "Dear Jesus," she prayed. "Please protect Petunia. And help us find her soon. Thank You for hearing our prayer, amen."

The family was silent for a moment, each person was thinking.

Suddenly Jason raised his hand. "Listen!" he said.

They listened carefully. Kyla could hear a vehicle in the distance and then the soft tweet of a bird singing in a nearby tree. And then she heard it. A dog was barking somewhere in the distance. It was Petunia!

They found the black dog in the hay field. Tall clover and grass towered over Petunia as she stood by a small hole, digging wildly. The dog wagged her tail when the family rushed toward her, but didn't quit digging. She would dig a few times, then bark. Dig and bark, dig and bark.

"What's that crazy thing doing?" Jason asked.

Kyla scooped Petunia into her arms.

"It's a mouse hole," Mrs. Hanton groaned. "She was chasing a mouse."

Petunia squirmed, trying to get free, and barked again.

"Great dog you've got there," Jason said, frowning at the dog. "Not only ugly, but dumb! Why didn't she come when she heard us calling?"

"It's not her fault," Kyla said, hugging Petunia tightly. "She doesn't know us yet.

But she will soon, and then she'll listen when we call."

Petunia barked one more time and then snuggled close to Kyla.

Dr. Marsh shook his head when he saw the dog. He didn't say anything as he checked Petunia's bald patch and skinny sides and her funny ear. But he kept shaking his head.

Finally he finished the examination.

"So what's wrong with my dog?" Kyla asked.

Dr. Marsh sighed again. "Mange," he said sharply. "And mites. And an infection of some sort—probably from having had puppies recently."

"Can it be treated?" Mrs. Hanton asked.

"I'm not finished," Dr. Marsh said. "She also has parasites and the worst case of fleas I've ever seen."

"We know," Jason groaned, scratching the back of his neck.

"And she has an inner ear infection," Dr. Marsh said. "And as abrasion to her cornea—that's her eye," he said, looking at Kyla. "Pugs' eyes stick out a bit, and they can hurt them easily."

"Will she get better?" Mrs. Hanton asked.

Dr. Marsh shrugged. "Maybe yes, maybe no," he said. "She's terribly thin and unhealthy. It's going to take someone a lot of time and effort and money to help her."

Kyla looked the vet in the eye. "You have to help Petunia," Kyla said firmly. "I just know she'll get better."

"Who's going to do all the work?" Dr. Marsh asked. "It's not going to be easy to help this dog."

"I'll do it," Kyla said. "She's my dog."

"Good," Dr. Marsh said. He smiled for the first time. "In that case, we had better get started. We have a lot to do before you take this creature home."

It was almost two hours before they were ready to go.

First Kyla helped the vet bathe Petunia with special flea shampoo. Then they cleaned her ears and put in some sticky yellow medication. They washed her dirty eyes, and put another kind of ointment in them. Dr. Marsh showed Kyla how to massage cream into the bald patch on Petunia's neck and how to trim her overgrown toenails.

"You'll have to help with this," Dr. Marsh said, turning to Mrs. Hanton. "Petunia will need these antibiotics twice a day." He showed Kyla's mother how to hold the dog and pop a pill down her throat.

Finally they were finished and on the way out the door.

"Don't forget her vitamins," Dr. Marsh called as Kyla carefully slipped the frayed collar and leash onto Petunia.

"I won't," Kyla promised.

"Now remember, feed her small meals frequently throughout the day," the vet continued. "Not too much at a time."

"I will," Kyla said.

"She needs to gain some weight, so give her good food," the vet instructed. "Like eggs. And milk. Cottage cheese. Canned dog food."

When the door to the clinic finally shut behind them, Jason gave a loud groan. "That dog is going to eat better than we do," he said. "Now, can we please go home?"

Kyla smiled as they got into the car. *I want to buy Petunia a new leash,* she thought, *and a new collar too. Maybe something fancy with sparkles on it. And tonight I can start to read the book on pugs. That will be fun!*

Yes, things were beginning to look up. Kyla finally had a dog of her own. In a few weeks Petunia would be a beautiful pug. Kyla closed her eyes, imagining it all. Maybe this dog would be everything she had dreamed about—wonderful and beautiful and smart.

CHAPTER

4

Petunia Meets Tuffy

Kyla's mother was upset at Petunia.

"She has absolutely no manners," Mrs. Hanton fussed when Kyla came home from school the next day. "She climbs right up the back of the couch! She sleeps on our kitchen chairs! And she barks all the time!"

Kyla rubbed special lotion onto the bald spot on Petunia's neck. "She's not barking now," Kyla said.

Just then Jason and their dad swung the entryway door open with a bang. Petunia jumped to her feet and began to bark loudly.

"Be quiet, Dog," Mrs. Hanton called.

"Shut up, Pesky," Jason said.

"Her name's not Pesky," Kyla snapped.

"It's Petunia."

"Petunia. Pesky," Jason said. "It's all the same to me." Petunia barked again.

Kyla's dad and mom looked at each other and shook their heads.

Kyla caught Petunia and finished rubbing lotion onto her neck. Her mother helped her put the eye ointment in Petunia's eye and the ear drops in her ears.

"Did you remember to give Petunia her medicine?" Kyla asked.

Mrs. Hanton nodded her head.

"Did you give her lots to eat?" Kyla looked in Petunia's bowl.

"I tried," Mrs. Hanton said. "But she only ate a few bites."

"Let me try," Kyla said.

Kyla put some fresh dog food in the bottom of the bowl and then poured some milk over top of it. "Come here, Petunia," Kyla called.

Petunia looked at the girl and wagged her tail. But instead of coming, she spun around and raced to the big sliding patio doors in the kitchen. The dog stopped, looked out the glass doors, and then began to yap.

"Here, Petunia," Kyla called again. "Come here, Girl."

Petunia wagged her tail but barked even louder.

Kyla walked over to the dog. "What are you barking at?" she asked.

Petunia licked Kyla's hand, wiggling happily. As Kyla watched a blue jay flew past the window, landing on the deck nearby.

Petunia really went wild now. She barked so hard her hind end bounced with each woof. Kyla could hardly keep from laughing. It was so funny! *Woof.* Petunia's ears bounced, and her back legs came right off the ground! *Woof, woof, woof.*

"Can't you make that dog be quiet!" Mr. Hanton called.

"Sorry, Dad," Kyla said. She picked up Petunia. "Shhhh," she whispered to the black dog. "You're making my dad mad."

Kyla carried the small dog to the entryway and showed her the dog food and milk. Petunia walked over to the dish and sniffed loudly. She looked at Kyla and wagged her tail once, as though thanking Kyla for the food.

"Come on, eat it," Kyla urged.

Petunia sniffed the food again and slowly took a bite.

"Good girl," Kyla said.

Petunia sighed and ate another bite. Then she suddenly twirled around and dashed out of the entryway. Kyla could hear the clicking of dog's feet on the kitchen floor, and then the barking started again.

"Be quiet!" Mrs. Hanton yelled.

Petunia didn't pause but barked even louder.

"Oh, dear," Kyla sighed. "I think I'd better take Petunia for a walk before she gets in really big trouble."

Petunia didn't seem to know how to behave when she went for a walk, either. She didn't lead very well. Instead of walking quietly beside Kyla, Petunia jumped one direction and then the other. She coughed and wheezed at the end of the leash, pulling every which way.

"Petunia, be good," Kyla ordered. She jerked on the leash impatiently, but Petunia didn't even seem to notice. Instead, Petunia watched as a black-and-white magpie flew past. Petunia charged off to follow the bird, reached the end of the leash, and tumbled over.

"Quit that, Silly," Kyla said. But Kyla had to smile to herself. Yes, Petunia was behaving badly, but Kyla could almost tell what the dog was thinking. Petunia's wagging tail and sparkling eyes said one thing: *This is a lot of fun! Much more fun than living in that boring place in the city!*

Kyla dragged Petunia back toward the house. They were almost at the deck when Petunia spotted something that really excited her.

It was Jason's old tomcat, Tuffy. Tuffy was

big and solid and wise. He didn't run when he saw the black dog come bouncing excitedly toward him. Instead, Tuffy narrowed his eyes and fluffed his tail and arched his back.

Kyla clung tightly to Petunia's leash. "Stop it, Petunia," Kyla yelled.

Petunia didn't glance at Kyla. Instead she whined and whimpered and tried to get over to the big cat. *Let's play. Let's be pals,* Petunia seemed to be saying.

Tuffy's glare said something different. *Come here and I'll rip you to shreds.*

"He'll hurt you," Kyla told Petunia.

Finally Petunia calmed down and stood straining at the end of the leash. Tuffy watched for a few moments and then slowly lowered his back. The cat's tail twitched a few times, but otherwise he stood still.

"Make friends, Petunia," Kyla ordered. "Tuffy will be nice to you if you're nice to him."

Petunia inched a bit closer to Tuffy. The cat's nose wrinkled, but he didn't move. Petunia crept another inch forward and then another.

Kyla held her breath, waiting to see what would happen.

Finally Petunia's and Tuffy's noses touched. They sniffed each other for a few moments, and then Petunia backed up a step, her tail happily wagging. Tuffy looked carefully at the dog and then seemed satisfied that there was no danger. The big cat sat down on the sidewalk and began to lick his paw.

Kyla didn't see exactly what happened. She just knew that suddenly Petunia jumped toward Tuffy with a loud bark. There was a snarl and hiss and then a wild yelp!

Yipe! Yipe! Yipe! Petunia squealed.

Tuffy stalked off, glaring over his shoulder. But Petunia was injured!

The little black dog rubbed her face frantically on her paws. She cried and whimpered and then cried some more. When Kyla looked at Petunia's face she could tell immediately that something was wrong. Petunia's left eye was shut, and several drops of bright red blood trickled down her face onto the grass.

Kyla scooped the dog up and rushed into the house. "Mom! Mom!" she hollered. "Come quick. Petunia's been hurt!"

Mrs. Hanton hurried into the entryway. "What happened?" she asked.

"I think Tuffy scratched Petunia's eye," Kyla said.

Kyla set Petunia down. The little dog curled into a small ball, her face tucked between her paws, looking totally miserable.

"Let me check it," Mrs. Hanton said.

Kyla held Petunia while her mother gently pried Petunia's eye open. The little dog whimpered but didn't struggle.

"Is she going to be all right?" Kyla asked.

Mrs. Hanton frowned. "I can see a cut on Petunia's eye," she said. "We're going to have to take her back to the vet."

"Again?" Kyla asked.

"Again!" Mrs. Hanton replied.

"Will she be blind?" Kyla asked.

Mrs. Hanton shrugged her shoulders. "I'm not a vet, so I don't know," she said. "I'll phone Dr. Marsh's office. Kyla, find that ointment we've been putting in Petunia's other eye. Maybe that will help take away some of the pain."

Kyla's heart was pounding as she tipped the bag full of Petunia's creams and lotions upside down onto the floor. What if Petunia's eye was seriously hurt? Would she be blind?

It's all my fault, Kyla thought. *If I hadn't let Petunia near Tuffy, this never would have happened.*

Kyla finally found the tube of eye ointment. She picked up Petunia and rushed to the kitchen. But as she hurried the last few steps, she prayed silently to herself. *Dear God, it's me, Kyla, again. Why did You let Petunia get hurt? Help her be a good dog, and help her be OK. Please. Because I love her a lot already.*

CHAPTER

5

Back to the Vet

"Back so soon?" Dr. Marsh asked when he saw Kyla and her parents with Petunia.

Kyla nodded her head glumly. "Our cat scratched Petunia's eye," she explained.

Dr. Marsh lifted Petunia up and set her on the examining table. He picked up a small flashlight and carefully checked the little dog's eye.

"Boy, your cat did a real number on her, didn't he?" Dr. Marsh said with a whistle.

"How bad is it?" Mr. Hanton asked.

The vet patted Petunia and was rewarded with a quick lick from the little dog. "It's serious," Dr. Marsh said. "But if we treat her eye carefully, I don't think she'll loose any vision. Did you put anything in Petunia's eye before bringing her in?"

Mrs. Hanton explained about the eye ointment.

"That was the right thing to do," Dr. Marsh said. "The ointment helped seal the cut shut and relieved some of the pain."

Kyla felt a bit better when she heard that.

"Now," Dr. Marsh continued. "I'll start her on a new ointment, and you'll have to bring her back in a few days so I can see how the eye is healing."

He quickly treated Petunia's eye and then patted the little dog again. Petunia wagged her tail.

"You have a really nice dog," Dr. Marsh said, looking at Kyla.

"Do you think so?" Kyla asked.

She looked at the funny little animal. Petunia looked terrible. She was skinny, and the bald spot on her neck seemed bigger than ever. Now she had one eye swollen shut.

"You're the first person who's ever told me anything nice about Petunia," Kyla said thoughtfully.

"I like her," Dr. Marsh said. "Many dogs struggle or fight when I treat them. But Petunia behaved like a real lady."

Mrs. Hanton laughed. "She's not a lady at home, let me tell you."

Kyla and her parents explained about Petunia's barking and climbing on the furniture and not coming when she was called.

"Well, that's different," Dr. Marsh said. "I was complimenting Petunia's character; that's something that you can't change very easily. Dogs, and people for that matter, are born with certain personalities. Some are shy. Some are inclined to be grumpy all the time. And some, like Petunia, are gentle and friendly. But how an animal is trained is a different thing. It sounds like no one has ever taken the time to train Petunia."

"It's not Petunia's fault," Kyla said. "No one took care of her."

"Yes, I suspect you're right," Dr. Marsh said. "Petunia may not have been actually abused, but she has been neglected. She wasn't fed or cared for properly. And it sounds as if she wasn't taught manners, either. That job is going to be yours."

"It sounds like hard work," Mr. Hanton said.

"Oh, it will be," Dr. Marsh agreed. "It could take months to teach Petunia manners. But I'm certain you can do it. I can tell that she's a smart little dog. Let me give you

PETUNIA, THE UGLY PUG

the address of a woman in Camrose who teaches obedience classes. You can take Petunia there when she's a bit healthier."

Dr. Marsh loaned Kyla a book on training dogs and waved as the family left the clinic. Kyla sighed as she climbed back in the car and snuggled Petunia on her knee.

"We have a lot of work to do," Kyla told Petunia.

When they got home, Kyla snapped the leash on Petunia's collar. "I wouldn't dare let you loose!" Kyla said. "You don't come when you're called, do you?"

Petunia wagged her tail happily.

They were almost at the doorstep when Tuffy stepped out from under the deck. He meowed and stretched, wanting some attention.

Petunia didn't see Tuffy with her good eye until they were only a few steps away.

This time Petunia didn't bark or try to run toward the cat. Instead the little dog sat down quickly by Kyla's feet. Petunia wagged her tail but didn't make any attempt to sniff Tuffy. Soon Tuffy got tired of watching the dog and slunk back under the deck. When the cat was out of sight, Petunia got to her feet and shook herself. Then she bounded up the steps and into the house.

"Maybe Petunia is a smart dog," Kyla said. "She didn't even get close to Tuffy this time."

Mr. Hanton snorted.

Mrs. Hanton shrugged her shoulders. "I guess we'll see," Kyla's mother said. "I guess we'll see."

When supper was finished, Kyla spent an hour or so reading Dr. Marsh's training book. Some of the words were long, but her mother helped her with them. Finally Kyla put the book down and turned to her mom. "This is a really good book," Kyla said. "And now I know what we should train Petunia to do first."

"What?" Mrs. Hanton asked.

"The first thing Petunia needs to learn is to come when she's called," Kyla said. "Do you think I can start tonight?"

Mrs. Hanton looked at Petunia, who was curled up on Kyla's lap, sound asleep. "Why don't you give her a day or so, until her eye feels better?" Mrs. Hanton suggested. "I would love to see Petunia's manners improve, but first I think we need to make sure she's feeling better."

Kyla nodded her head slowly.

Suddenly there was a burst of noise from the front room as Jason flicked channels on the TV. There was the sound of gunfire and people yelling.

Petunia sat up on Kyla's knee and barked.

"Be quiet," Kyla said, grabbing the dog's collar so she couldn't jump off her lap.

"Turn the TV down, Jason," Mrs. Hanton ordered.

"No, turn the TV off," Mr. Hanton called over the noise in the front room. "You know we don't watch that type of TV show."

Petunia barked again.

Jason grumbled and then clicked off the TV. "Stupid dog," Jason said as he walked past the group.

"Petunia's a good dog," Kyla said quickly. "She just didn't like your TV show."

"Why did you get the dumb thing?" Jason said. "All she does is bark."

"Jason," Mrs. Hanton warned.

"What?" Jason said. "I'm just telling the truth."

"I love Petunia," Kyla said, hugging the little dog.

Petunia wagged her tail happily and tried to lick Jason.

The boy frowned at Petunia. "Look at her," Jason said. "That must be the ugliest dog in Alberta. Maybe the ugliest dog in all of Canada. She could win an ugly-dog contest! No one in their right mind would want a monster like that around."

"That's enough," Mr. Hanton said sharply. "Jason, you can go down to your room for a while. You know that you're not allowed to talk like that."

"Fine," Jason said. "I was going there anyhow."

In a moment they heard Jason's bedroom door slam shut. Petunia wagged her tail and then curled back up on Kyla's lap.

Mr. Hanton looked at the little dog and then at Kyla. "Are you certain this is the dog you want?" he asked kindly.

Kyla nodded her head.

"She's going to be a lot of work," Mr. Hanton continued. "You heard Dr. Marsh. He said it could be months before she begins to behave herself."

"She'll learn to be good, Daddy," Kyla said. "I'll teach her."

"Well, I think that we should phone that woman in Camrose," Mr. Hanton said. "I think that some obedience classes would be a big help for you both."

"Maybe we should send Jason to obedience school," Kyla said, looking toward Jason's bedroom door.

"Kyla," Mr. Hanton said. "Now *you* are talking unkindly."

"He started it," Kyla said. She stood up,

holding Petunia. "I'm sorry, Dad. Of course I'd like to take Petunia to obedience school. It sounds like fun."

I just hope no one blames me for the way Petunia looks, Kyla thought, feeling a bit ashamed of her thoughts. *But Jason was right. Petunia is really ugly.* Then Kyla started to pray. *Please help Petunia become the perfect dog, Jesus, and if You don't mind— could You change her really soon?*

CHAPTER
6

Petunia Goes to Obedience School

"Hi," Kyla said, smiling at the girl who stood nearby. The girl's golden retriever strained at its leash, trying to sniff Petunia.

The girl smiled back. "What kind of dog is that?" she asked.

"Petunia's a pug," Kyla explained. She looked around the Camrose arena. Twelve pairs of dogs and handlers stood around talking, waiting for the first obedience class to begin. Petunia was the smallest dog there.

"I thought pugs were creamy colored, with black faces," the girl said, still looking at Petunia.

"Most of them are," Kyla explained. "But some pugs are black."

"Why doesn't she have hair on her neck?" the girl asked.

"It's growing back," Kyla said. "Petunia had mange."

"Mange!" The girl backed up a step, pulling the golden retriever with her. "That's awful! Why, they shoot coyotes if they have mange! Maybe you'll spread it to the other dogs."

"No," Kyla said quickly. "My vet said that Petunia is OK now. Look, her hair is growing back and—"

The girl was gone.

Kyla looked down at Petunia and sighed. Petunia *was* getting better. The bald spot was partly covered with short, bristly hairs. She was still skinny, but at least every rib and hipbone didn't show. Her eyes were bright, and her ears stood properly. She was happy and lively. Yes, Kyla could tell that Petunia was much, much better.

But she still looked weird.

"Maybe I should have gotten another dog," Kyla muttered. But then Kyla felt ashamed of herself. *She's my dog,* Kyla thought, *and she needs me to love her.*

"Attention, Class," the instructor called loudly. "May I have your attention, please?"

The group became quiet, except for a large Rottweiler in the corner that barked loudly every few seconds, almost pulling his handler off his feet.

"My name is Beth Warren," the woman said. "I will be teaching your class for the next ten weeks. Before we start, I want to tell you that you all have a lot of work ahead of you. Please don't get discouraged when things don't seem to go well at first. By the end of the next few months, I think you will see a huge improvement in your dogs' behavior."

Mrs. Warren beckoned to a teenage girl with a tan cocker spaniel standing quietly on the other side of the room. "This is Megan Brown and her dog, Regal. They took our obedience class last summer and are working toward their CD title in obedience at the open dog shows. I asked Megan if she would bring Regal here today to show you what your dogs can do if you work steadily with them."

The teenager smiled and rubbed the cocker spaniel's silky ears.

"Are you ready, Megan?" Mrs. Warren asked.

"Yes," Megan said, nodding her head.

"All right. Walk forward please."

"Regal, heel," the teenager said. She stepped forward briskly. The cocker spaniel sprang to its feet and began to trot down the arena, keeping close to her owner. When

Megan stopped walking, the tan dog sat down promptly without being told to do so. They walked up and down the arena, and then they ran up and down the arena. Every time Megan stopped, the dog sat down. Every time she moved, the dog trotted briskly by her side.

"You better watch this," Kyla said, looking at Petunia.

But Petunia was sound asleep, snoring through her flat pug nose.

Next Megan showed how Regal would sit and stay without moving for several minutes, and then lie and stay even longer. At the end they did a perfect recall—coming when called.

"Petunia, wake up," Kyla said, poking Petunia with one finger. "This is important."

Petunia grunted but didn't open her eyes.

"Regal needs to place in one more class, and we will have our CD title. CD stands for 'companion dog,' " the teenager explained when they finished. "I'm very proud of Regal; she's a wonderful dog!"

"Could we do something like that?" the man with the barking Rottweiler asked.

Mrs. Warren nodded her head. "Most dogs can earn their CD title if you work with them daily. Only registered dogs can enter real dog trials, but nonregistered dogs can still enter fun trials. If anyone is interested, please see me after the class. Now, we need to begin."

Mrs. Warren began explaining how to teach your dog to lead properly. Kyla listened eagerly. It didn't sound too hard. Petunia was to lead on her left side. Kyla was to pat her leg and talk to Petunia whenever she was looking at her and paying attention. But anytime Petunia turned away and quit looking, Kyla was to turn and run the other direction.

"Won't that hurt them?" a woman asked, gently patting her own dog on the head.

"Well, it will surprise them," Mrs. Warren said. "That's the whole point. We want to teach your dogs that if they watch you and pay attention, things will be fine. But if they take their eyes off you, they'll get themselves in trouble."

At first Petunia paid attention to everyone and everything except Kyla. Every time Petunia looked away, Kyla would run the other direction. Poor Petunia would hit the end of the leash, be jerked forward, and then turn and run after Kyla.

"Stupid dog," Kyla muttered when it happened again and then again.

Petunia wagged her tail hesitantly.

Kyla was panting and tired and almost ready to give up when it happened. Petunia heeled up and down the whole length of the arena and didn't take her eyes off Kyla—even when they passed the barking Rottweiler.

"Good job," Mrs. Warren called to Kyla.

"We did it!" Kyla said. She patted the little dog and made a fuss over her. Petunia bounced around happily and licked Kyla's hand.

"Very good, everyone," Mrs. Warren called. "Now, I have some written instructions for you to take home this week. It's important that you work on these exercises every day, or your dogs won't improve. Does anyone have any questions?"

A woman with a Doberman pinscher raised her hand. "Isn't this cruel to our animals? It seems that we're causing them pain by jerking on the leashes."

Mrs. Warren nodded her head. "Yes, I agree that it probably does hurt the dogs a little to have their leashes jerked. But look at the other options. Dogs that are poorly trained and out of control have terrible lives. Many are put to sleep because their owners cannot handle them. Many are abandoned or taken to the pound. Many are treated roughly or ignored because their owners are angry with them. If you treat your dogs fairly and correct them only when they do wrong, and treat them kindly when they do right, they will learn how to behave. So I believe that obedience training is actually kind. It will make your and your dogs' lives better."

Kyla thought about that on the way home. "I think Mrs. Warren is right," Kyla told her father. "Dogs like that big Rottweiler—or Petunia—aren't any fun to have around if they don't behave."

"Tell me about it," Mr. Hanton said with a smile.

"Petunia is smart; I can tell," Kyla said. "She really improved today."

"That's good," Mr. Hanton said.

"Dad," Kyla said, and then hesitated.

"What?"

"Do you think— I would like to take Petunia to some obedience competitions at a dog show. Could I do that one day?" Kyla asked.

Mr. Hanton looked surprised. "I don't know," he said. "I don't know anything about dog shows."

"Mrs. Warren said that any registered dog can compete. And Petunia's registered."

"Well," Mr. Hanton said, "we can at least get more information."

Kyla was smiling as she climbed into bed that night. She had been getting frustrated with Petunia, but now things were beginning to look better. Maybe God had given her the dog of her dreams after all.

My dog, Kyla thought, as she closed her eyes, *is going to be perfect.*

CHAPTER
7

Kyla
Loses Her Temper

Petunia wasn't perfect after all. And Kyla was beginning to get tired of the dog's many problems.

"You're leading better," Kyla grumbled later that week after practicing in the yard with Petunia. "But you're still a big brat!"

Petunia barked loudly as a flock of birds flew overhead.

Kyla jerked on the leash, turning Petunia away from the birds. "You bark too much," Kyla complained. "And you still won't come when I call. Aren't you ever going to be good?"

Petunia jumped up and put her paws on Kyla's legs, wagging her tail happily.

"Everybody's always mad at you," Kyla said. "Maybe they're right. Maybe you are a bad dog."

Petunia licked Kyla's hand.

Kyla sighed. "Come on, Silly. Let's go see what Mom's making for supper."

Petunia trotted by Kyla's left side as they walked up to the house. They were almost at the doorstep when a loud howl stopped them both in their tracks.

Tuffy and a strange orange cat raced out from under the steps. The orange cat ran a few feet and then whirled around to fight with Tuffy. Both cats shrieked and hissed angrily.

Petunia completely forgot her manners. She darted toward the two cats, pulling the leash out of Kyla's hands.

"Petunia!" Kyla yelled. "Come back."

Petunia didn't pause, but raced toward the cats, barking loudly.

Kyla could hardly believe her eyes. Was Petunia going to get hurt again? She was finally healed after her first encounter with an angry cat, and now the crazy dog was chasing *two* cats!

"Petunia!"

Petunia ran straight toward the cats, barking loudly. Tuffy hissed and spat, first at the orange cat and then at Petunia. The orange cat jumped out of the way in time and ran off across the lawn. But Petunia didn't move quickly enough and was scratched on her chest and front leg.

"Petunia, come!" Kyla yelled. But she knew it wouldn't help, because Petunia never came when she was called.

Fortunately Petunia sat down and held her scratched leg up in the air. She was motionless for a moment, and Kyla was able to catch hold of her leash before Petunia sprang forward to chase the cats again.

Kyla was both frightened and angry. "Bad dog!" she yelled. She jerked on Petunia's leash. Hard. "You never listen to me, do you?"

A wave of anger and frustration rushed over Kyla. All the annoying things that Petunia did came to her mind—the barking, the disobedience, the many times Petunia ignored Kyla. Kyla was so angry that she didn't even stop to think. She raised her hand and hit the little dog. She hit Petunia once, and then again.

Petunia didn't struggle but flattened herself against the ground.

Kyla raised her hand to smack Petunia

again and then stopped. Petunia's big brown eyes were full of surprise and hurt. But her tail wagged once, slowly and hesitantly.

Kyla's eyes filled with tears. "What am I doing?" she cried.

Kyla bent over to pick Petunia up. Petunia crouched even lower to the ground, as if she was afraid Kyla was going to hit her again.

Kyla really began to cry now. "Why did I do that?" Kyla whispered. "I'm really, really sorry, Petunia. I was just so scared and mad and—and—"

She picked up Petunia and rushed into the house.

Once Kyla was certain that Petunia's scratches weren't serious, she left the dog in the kitchen and hurried into her bedroom. Kyla shut the door behind her and sank down onto her bed.

She cried for a long time. Kyla felt terrible. She was ashamed, embarrassed, and sad. She was angry at Petunia for not being the perfect dog, and she was angry at herself for hitting the animal.

"I shouldn't have a pet if I act like that," Kyla whispered to herself. "In fact, I wish I didn't have Petunia."

Finally Kyla quit crying. She lay quietly on her bed, staring up at the ceiling. What should she do?

She could hear Petunia bark in the distance. For once Kyla didn't care when Jason yelled at the dog. "Shut up!" he hollered.

At least Jason doesn't hit her, Kyla thought sadly. *He just calls her names.* It was quiet for a moment and then the barking started again.

I should pray, Kyla finally thought. *But I don't think God would want to talk to someone like me. I know I've been bad. And God doesn't like bad people.*

"Kyla!" Mr. Hanton called from the kitchen. "Come and get your dog."

Kyla sighed and swung her feet over the edge of the bed. *What an awful day,* Kyla thought, slowly getting to her feet. *Petunia is a terrible dog, and I'm a terrible person.*

Kyla was quiet all evening. She didn't have anything to say during supper or when she dried the dishes. And instead of spending time in the evening with Petunia, she put the little dog in her dog carrier and hurried off to her room.

After a while there was a knock on

Kyla's bedroom door. Kyla sat up quickly.

"Who is it?" she asked.

"It's Mom," Mrs. Hanton called. "May I come in?"

"I guess so," Kyla said.

Mrs. Hanton sat down on the edge of the bed and smiled at Kyla. Kyla tried to smile back, but it wasn't a very happy smile.

"Come on, Kyla," Mrs. Hanton finally said. "What's wrong?"

"Wrong?" Kyla said. "Nothing's wrong."

"Of course there is," Mrs. Hanton said. "You look like you've just lost your best friend."

Kyla had to blink very hard now. Her mom was right, even though she didn't know it. Kyla *had* lost her best friend.

"I think we should find Petunia another home," Kyla finally said in a rush.

"What?"

"I'm sure someone would like her," Kyla continued. "Maybe the dog trainer from Camrose would take her. Maybe she could teach Petunia to be a good dog."

Mrs. Hanton scratched her head. "What are you talking about?" she asked.

"I don't want a dog anymore," Kyla said, studying a loose button on the front of her shirt. "Especially Petunia—so we should find her another home where someone would take good care of her."

Kyla twisted the button around and around with one finger.

Mrs. Hanton sighed and put her hand on Kyla's shoulder. "OK," Kayla's mother said, "spill the beans. What happened today?"

"Nothing," Kyla said. She twirled the button the other direction.

Mrs. Hanton didn't move. "Talk to me, Kyla," she said. "Obviously something has upset you today. Tell me about it."

"I can't," Kyla whispered. "It's too bad."

"Listen, Kyla," her mother said. "We need to talk about things, even when they're bad. Perhaps *especially* when they're bad. That's how problems get solved."

"If I tell you, then you'll be mad at me too," Kyla said. She yanked the button hard and watched as the thread broke. The button skittered across the bedroom floor and disappeared out of sight behind her dresser.

"I might be angry," Mrs. Hanton said. "But I'll still love you. Now, tell me what happened."

Kyla didn't answer.

Mrs. Hanton waited for a moment and

then raised her eyebrows. "Kyla," she repeated, "tell me what happened."

"OK," Kyla said in a rush. "I hit Petunia. I hit her hard. She made me mad, so I just hit her! And now she's scared of me, and God's mad at me, and you're going to be mad at me too! I've done everything wrong, and I just don't know what to do about it."

Kyla looked down at the floor. She didn't want to see the look on her mom's face. Kyla knew that her mother was going to be upset. Very, very upset.

CHAPTER

8

Forgiveness

It was quiet for a moment. Finally Kyla looked up and studied her mom's face. "Aren't you going to yell at me?" Kyla asked.

Mrs. Hanton shook her head. "No," she said.

"Are you mad at me?" Kyla asked.

Mrs. Hanton put her arm around Kyla's shoulder. "Honey, I'm not happy that you hit Petunia, but I still love you."

Kyla let her breath out. "Oh, good," she said.

Mrs. Hanton smiled faintly. "But we do need to talk about your problem. In fact," she continued, "I think you have several problems."

Kyla nodded her head.

"Kyla, Petunia *has* been a difficult dog. And none of us have given you much help with her," Mrs. Hanton said. "We're always mad at Petunia and expecting you to make her behave. So first of all, I want to say I'm sorry, and I'll try to help you with Petunia more." Mrs. Hanton smiled into Kyla's eyes.

Kyla looked surprised. "Really?" she asked.

"Really," Mrs. Hanton said. "Now, let's talk about your hitting Petunia."

Kyla sighed. "I can't believe I did it," she said sadly. "I mean, I love Petunia, really I do. But sometimes she makes me so angry."

"Does she?" Mrs. Hanton asked.

"Uh-huh," Kyla nodded. "Petunia's always getting into trouble. Today she ran away and started chasing the cats, and I was scared she was going to get hurt again. Mom, I just want Petunia to listen to me and not be so bad!"

Mrs. Hanton nodded her head, listening.

"I became really angry, and I hit her," Kyla said. She paused, and then spoke sadly. "I shouldn't even own a dog anymore."

Mrs. Hanton sighed. "Kyla, everyone gets angry sometimes," she said. "Anger is just a feeling, and feelings aren't bad. You aren't a bad person for feeling angry, and it's not your feelings that caused the problem. It's what you did with your feelings."

"Like hitting Petunia," Kyla said gloomily.

"Yes, like hitting Petunia," Mrs. Hanton said. "You knew it was wrong to hit your pet. Just like it would be wrong for me to punch someone because I was angry."

"You'd never do that!" Kyla said, almost smiling in spite of herself. She tried to imagine her mom with a pair of boxing gloves on, jabbing at the air, trying to hit someone.

"No, I hope I would never do anything like that," Mrs. Hanton agreed. "But that doesn't mean that I don't ever get angry."

"But I couldn't stop myself from hitting Petunia," Kyla said.

"Yes, you could have," Mrs. Hanton said firmly. "Being angry doesn't mean that we have to act a certain way. Everyone needs to learn to find way to handle his or her temper. Some people count to ten before they act. Some people walk away from the problem and wait to calm down before they do anything."

"Does that really help?" Kyla asked doubtfully.

"It helps me," Mrs. Hanton said. "When

I'm angry, I try to get away from the problem for a few moments and pray. I ask God to help me think of good ways to handle my anger."

"Give me an example," Kyla said.

"Why, just today I was angry at Jason," Mrs. Hanton said with a faint smile. "He's at a difficult age right now, and I was almost ready to choke him! But I went to the bathroom and—"

"The bathroom?" Kyla interrupted.

"The bathroom," Mrs. Hanton repeated. "You see, I can lock the bathroom door, and no one can come in while I'm calming down! And then I prayed for God to give me some ideas on handling Jason."

"Did it help?" Kyla asked.

"Yes, it did," Mrs. Hanton said. "Now, do you think that you could plan to do something like that next time you're angry?"

"Do you think I should go into the bathroom?" Kyla asked.

Mrs. Hanton smiled. "Maybe," she said. "Or maybe just go to your room. You need to get away from Petunia when you're feeling really frustrated with her."

Kyla slowly nodded her head. "OK, Mom," she said. "I'll try that next time." Kyla got up from her bed and stretched. "May I go tell

Petunia I'm sorry before I go to sleep?" she asked.

"Sure," Mrs. Hanton said. "But first I want to discuss one more thing with you."

"What, Mom?"

"You mentioned that God was mad at you for hitting Petunia," Mrs. Hanton said.

"Oh," Kyla stopped. "I guess I did say that."

"Well," Mrs. Hanton said. "God does want us to treat animals kindly, but don't forget that no matter how awful we behave, God still love us. He hates the bad things we do, but He loves us anyhow."

"Really?"

"Really," Mrs. Hanton said. "Kyla, we all do bad things sometimes. Even Jesus' special friends we read about in the Bible made mistakes. Like Peter or King David or Moses. But when they asked God to forgive them, He did. And God will forgive you when you make mistakes too. So next time you do something wrong, don't forget that God still loves you and wants to forgive you. OK?"

"OK," Kyla said.

Kyla actually felt happy as she skipped down the hallway. Things didn't look nearly as terrible now as they had a few hours before.

Petunia was glad to get out of her dog carrier. She bounced out and shook herself and licked Kyla's hand.

I forgive you, Petunia seemed to be saying. *Now, let's go find something to do.*

Suddenly Petunia's ears pointed ahead. She took a quick step forward, but Kyla caught her in time and picked her up.

"No barking, Silly Girl," Kyla said. "Come with me."

Kyla carried Petunia into the bathroom, scratching her ears as they went.

"This," Kyla said, looking around, "is where I'm going to come next time I'm angry at you. So why don't you try to behave a bit better, hey? I don't want to spend that much time in the bathroom; it's kind of boring."

Kyla sat down on the sink counter. Petunia wagged her tail cheerfully and twisted around to lick Kyla again.

Suddenly Petunia spotted herself in the mirror.

The little dog's ears shot up in surprise. Her forehead wrinkled with amazement, and the hair on the back of her neck began to bristle.

Petunia stared at her own reflection in the mirror, but she didn't seem to like what she saw. The little dog began to growl softly. The soft growl got louder and louder, and then Petunia started to bark.

Watch out, Petunia seemed to be saying. *There's a strange enemy dog here in the bathroom!*

"Mom! Dad!" Kyla called. "Come look at Petunia!"

Soon the whole Hanton family was in the bathroom laughing at Petunia's behavior. They laughed even louder when Kyla put Petunia down, and the little dog ran straight across the counter and crashed into the mirror.

"So that's how pugs get flat faces!" Jason laughed.

Petunia scratched at the mirror, trying to reach the dangerous dog she could see just a few inches away!

"Jason!" Kyla giggled.

"I always thought they got flat faces from chasing parked cars," Jason continued. "But I guess I was wrong."

Finally Mrs. Hanton picked Petunia up. "Enough of this," Mrs. Hanton said. "She's spitting all over the clean mirror. Out you go, Miss Watchdog."

The family was still chuckling as Kyla carried Petunia out of the bathroom.

"I told you we should call her Pesky," Jason called. "She's the peskiest thing I've ever seen."

Kyla hugged Petunia before tucking her back into her dog carrier for the night. "Sleep tight, Silly," Kyla said. "I love you. Even if you are a goof."

Kyla smiled as she climbed into her own bed. *Dear God,* she prayed silently, smiling up at the ceiling. *It's me, Kyla. I guess Petunia isn't going to be perfect after all. That's OK. I still love her. Please forgive me for hitting Petunia today.* Kyla sighed and rolled over in bed. *And thank You, Jesus, for loving me even when I'm not perfect either.*

CHAPTER

9

Petunia Learns to Obey

"Today we're going to work on our re-calls," Mrs. Warren said. "You'll need your long leash and some dog treats. Now, could I borrow someone's dog to show you how a proper recall is done?"

Kyla quickly raised her hand.

"Thank you," Mrs. Warren said. The woman snapped a long soft leash onto Petunia's collar and patted the little dog. "Now, I'll have you hold Petunia in place while I back up a bit."

When Mrs. Warren was at the end of the leash, she pulled a dog treat out of her pocket. "It's very simple," the woman said. "I'll call 'Petunia' and then 'come.' If she doesn't come right away, I'll jerk the leash. As soon as she moves my direction, I quit pulling. When Petunia gets here, I give her a treat. Now watch, and we'll teach this little dog something new."

Petunia stared across the arena, totally ignoring the group. Mrs. Warren bent over. "Petunia," she called. "Come."

Petunia didn't move. There was a short pause, and then Mrs. Warren snapped the leash firmly. Petunia was surprised. She jumped to her feet. Mrs. Warren called again, and when Petunia didn't move, she jerked the leash a second time. Petunia looked around the room and then trotted over to the woman.

"Good dog," Mrs. Warren said, popping the treat into Petunia's mouth. "Very good."

Petunia wagged her tail wildly.

"Now, let's see you try," Mrs. Warren said, looking at Kyla.

To Kyla's amazement, Petunia came the first time Kyla called. Kyla gave her a reward and patted the little dog.

"Don't expect all your dogs to respond this quickly," Mrs. Warren said. "Kyla has it easy."

"What did you mean?" Kyla asked when the pairs separated to work on their recalls.

"Petunia is very willing," Mrs. Warren said, rubbing Petunia's ears. "She's a very smart little dog, and she's beginning to really pay attention to you. I think she would do very well in obedience competition. Have you thought of working towards your CD?"

Kyla nodded shyly.

Mrs. Warren smiled. "Good," she said. "We can talk about it after class."

Kyla was excited on the way home. "Petunia is doing really well," she told her mother. "I want to train her for obedience trials. Mrs. Warren said she'd be good at it."

"Well, you've got a lot of work ahead of you," Mrs. Hanton said.

"And guess what?" Kyla continued. "Mrs. Warren told me how to stop Petunia from barking!"

"Really?" Mrs. Hanton looked doubtful.

"Really, Mom. That's Petunia's worst habit—barking all the time. And it drives us all crazy!" Kyla said.

"So what are we supposed to do?" Mrs. Hanton asked.

"Buy a squirt gun," Kyla said with a grin.

"What?"

"I'm supposed to say 'Quiet' when Petunia barks. If she quits barking, we don't do anything. But if she keeps barking, we're supposed to squirt her with the squirt gun!" Kyla explained.

Mrs. Hanton began to laugh.

"Honest, Mom," Kyla said. "But we have to do it every time she barks. That means I have to carry the squirt gun with me, so I'm always ready to spray her."

Mrs. Hanton grinned back at Kyla. "OK," she said. "It's worth a try. Tomorrow morning I'll buy a squirt gun. Maybe we can change a certain little dog's mind about barking all the time!"

Mrs. Hanton bought three squirt guns. "One is to keep in the kitchen," she explained. "And one is for the entryway. And one," she said, pointing to Kyla, "is for you to carry with you."

"Cool!" Jason said. He rubbed his hands together. "Now this is my idea of dog training!"

"Jason!" Kyla wailed. "You can't squirt Petunia if she's being good. Promise me! Mrs. Warren said she'll get confused if we don't do things right."

"What are you talking about?" Jason said innocently. "Don't you trust me?"

"No!" Kyla said loudly. "Please, Jason. Promise me that you'll be good."

Mrs. Hanton frowned at Jason. Finally

he sighed. "OK, OK," he said. "I won't squirt the dopey thing if she behaves herself. But I get to give her a blast when she barks. Right?"

They didn't have long to wait. Kyla opened the dog carrier and let Petunia out. Petunia immediately galloped up the entryway steps and tore over to the big patio doors. She began to bark loudly.

"Petunia, quiet!" Kyla yelled. The dog didn't even pause.

But when the stream of water from Kyla's water gun sprayed Petunia on the shoulder, she jumped into the air and stared around the room. *Where did that come from?* Petunia seemed to be asking.

Kyla laughed.

Petunia was quiet for a moment, and then a bird flew past the window. Petunia raised her head and barked again.

"Petunia, quiet," Kyla said. Petunia barked again.

This time the dog was squirted by two different water guns.

Petunia sprang sideways and looked around the room. She seemed confused. Kyla bit her lip, trying to keep from giggling.

"Bull's-eye!" Jason snickered.

Petunia looked at Kyla and Jason and

then around the room. She shook herself and sat down on her haunches.

It was quiet in the kitchen for a moment. Then Petunia got to her feet and trotted around the corner. When she was out of sight she began to bark again.

Jason grinned and picked up the water gun.

"Petunia, quiet!" Kyla called. The barking stopped.

By the end of the week Petunia didn't bark anymore.

"I kind of miss all the excitement," Jason grumbled one evening after supper.

"You just miss squirting her!" Kyla said, rubbing Petunia's ears.

"It was fun, wasn't it?" Jason said. "It's too bad she's so smart—uh—so boring now."

"Petunia is smart, isn't she?" Kyla said.

Jason didn't answer. He picked up a taco chip from the kitchen table, dipped it in salsa, and ate it. Petunia looked at Jason and trotted around the kitchen table to stand by him. She wagged her tail hopefully.

"Want a snack, Pesky?" Jason asked.

"She won't like salsa," Kyla said. "It's too hot."

Petunia wagged her tail faster.

"She's hungry," Jason said. He scooped a

generous amount of salsa onto a taco chip. "Here, Little Doggy. Have a treat."

He reached down with the taco chip.

Petunia ate it in one bite and then wagged her tail for more.

Jason looked at Kyla and raised his eyebrows. "See," he said, "she knows good food when she tastes it."

"I didn't think dogs would eat spicy stuff like that," Kyla said.

"Let's see what she thinks of Dad's extra-hot salsa," Jason said. He opened the other jar of salsa and scooped some onto a taco chip.

"No!" Kyla said sharply.

But when Jason passed the chip to Petunia, she ate it eagerly.

"Cool!" Jason said. He patted the dog on the head. Petunia licked her lips and begged for more.

When Mrs. Hanton came into the kitchen a few minutes later, she saw a strange sight. Petunia sat on Jason's lap, eating the left-over onions and green peppers and salsa as fast as Jason could pass them to her.

"Look, Mom!" Jason called. "Isn't this neat? Petunia isn't such a bad dog after all."

"Enough!" Mrs. Hanton ordered. "You'll

have to clean up the mess if she gets sick, Jason."

"She won't get sick," Jason said. "After all, Dad eats this stuff all the time." But he patted Petunia one more time and then set her down on the floor.

Petunia wagged her tail again for Jason, thanking him for the snack, and then trotted around to where Kyla was sitting. Petunia sprang up on Kyla's lap, turned around once, and settled down for a nap.

"You're lucky," Jason said, standing up and stretching.

"Am I?" Kyla asked.

"Yeah," Jason said. "I wish—" He stopped and turned around.

"What do you wish?" Kyla asked.

"Ah, nothing," Jason said. "Look, I got some math homework to do. See you later, Petunia."

Jason left the room. Mrs. Hanton and Kyla grinned at each other. Kyla's mom shrugged her shoulders. "Well, what do you know?" Mrs. Hanton said. "It looks like Petunia is starting to grow on Jason."

"Wow!" Kyla said.

"Who knows," Mrs. Hanton continued. "Maybe Jason will want a pug of his own one day."

CHAPTER
10

Petunia Goes to the Dog Show

Kyla looked around the dog show in amazement. She had never seen so many dogs in her life! She carefully guided Petunia past the rows of dog cages and carriers.

"Look!" Kyla said, nudging her mother with one elbow. They watched as a woman used a blow-drier to fluff up her white poodle's already perfect ears. Another woman stood nearby, brushing a smaller dog.

"I'm glad Petunia has short hair like me," Kyla whispered. Petunia looked up at Kyla and wagged her tail.

Mrs. Hanton didn't answer. She seemed frazzled as she carried the empty dog carrier in one hand, and two chairs and a bag of supplies in the other.

"Let's set our stuff here," Kyla said, spotting an empty place.

Kyla sat down on one of their folding chairs and snuggled Petunia up on her knee. She turned the pages of the dog-show catalogue until she came to the section on obedience.

"Here we are, Mom," Kyla said, pointing to the middle of the page. "Obedience 'Novice A' class. Here are our names, Kyla Hanton and Black Petunia Lass."

Mrs. Hanton looked over Kyla's shoulder. "Good," she said. "We've got an hour before your class starts."

"Look how many other dogs are entered!" Kyla suddenly wailed. "There are twenty-two dogs! We don't stand a chance."

Mrs. Hanton shook her head. "Everyone can pass," she reminded Kyla. "All you need is a good score, and you're part way to earning your title."

"Oh," Kyla said, "right." She scratched Petunia's ear.

Petunia didn't seem the least bit bothered by all the noise and confusion going on around them. Instead she sighed, closed her eyes, and fell asleep. In a few moments the little dog was snoring loudly.

Petunia must really trust me, Kyla thought. *She's not worried about all these other dogs, is she? Dear God, help me trust You too. I don't have to win, but please keep us both safe, and help us do our best.*

Kyla's heart was pounding by the time their class was announced. She paced and fretted as she watched the dogs ahead of her perform. Some seemed to move absolutely perfectly, not leaving their owners' side for a second. Other dogs made terrible mistakes. One ran out of the ring when let loose for the recall. Another dog bit the judge when he touched it for the stand-for examination.

"At least you won't bite anyone, will you?" Kyla said, petting Petunia.

"Next is Kyla Hanton and her pug, Black Petunia Lass," the announcer called. "Petunia is our only pug working in obedience today."

The crowd clapped politely.

Kyla bent over and patted Petunia one last time and then cleared her throat. She tried to remember everything that Mrs. Warren had told her. *Walk briskly, but not too fast. Give your command only once. Don't pat Petunia until you have finished the exercise.*

Kyla was in the ring now, Petunia sitting obediently on her left side. The judge smiled at Kyla and marked something on her piece of paper.

"Good morning," the judge said.

"Good morning," Kyla squeaked.

"Don't be nervous," the judge said kindly. "I'm certain you'll do just fine."

Kyla took a big breath and tried to clear her head.

"Ready?" the judge said. "Walk forward, please."

"Petunia, heel," Kyla ordered, stepping forward. Petunia jumped to her feet and began to trot briskly down the ring beside Kyla.

The next few minutes went by in a blur to Kyla. First there was the heel on leash, where they followed the judge's directions up and down the mat.

Next there was the stand-for examination, where Petunia was to stand quietly while the judge examined her. That seemed to go well—the only thing that moved on Petunia was her wagging tail.

"Heel free," the judge announced next. This was one of the parts that Kyla had been dreading. She unsnapped the leash from Petunia's collar and set it aside. Now they went through the heeling pattern again, this time with Petunia following beside Kyla without a leash to guide her.

That part seemed to go all right, too, although Petunia did get a bit farther away on some of the corners. But at least she didn't run off across the ring and disappear from sight.

"Recall," the judge ordered when the free heeling was finished.

We're just about finished, Kyla thought, taking a deep breath. She put Petunia on a sitting stay and walked forward. The judge made her wait for a moment and then nodded her head.

"Petunia, come!" Kyla called firmly.

But then something terrible happened. Just when Petunia stood up to move, a loud, howling screech blared from the announcer's loudspeaker! Everyone put their hands to their ears and spun around! Everyone, that is, except Kyla.

Kyla had to see what Petunia would do. Would she stop? Would she run away? Finally the loud noise quit.

But Petunia didn't stop. Instead, she trotted down the mat straight toward Kyla.

The judge turned her attention back to the pair, and her face brightened when she saw the little pug sitting quietly in front of Kyla. "Good job!" the judge said happily.

The judge nodded. Kyla bent down and began patting Petunia. They had done it!

The last portion of the class seemed easier. Kyla and Petunia went into the ring with the other dogs for the one-minute sit-stays, and the three-minute down-stays. Several dogs moved, but Petunia wasn't one of them. When they were out of the class, Mrs. Hanton hugged Kyla and patted Petunia and praised them for the good job they did.

"Wonderful work," Mrs. Hanton said. "I am so proud of the two of you."

In a few minutes the judge spoke over the loudspeaker. "This was a very good group," the judge announced. "We had sixteen dogs pass their Novice A class. That is an unusually high number."

The judge called all the qualifying dogs into the ring. Petunia was one of them.

"Now, in third place, we have Carl Jahns and his black lab, Mr. Bo Man, with a score of 192 points," the judge announced.

There was applause as the judge presented a long white ribbon to the pair.

"In second place we have Hillary Young and her border collie, Busytown Mac, with a score of 193 points."

The applause was louder now.

Kyla tried not to care about the last ribbon. She didn't need a ribbon to be happy, she reminded herself.

"And for first place we have a two-way tie," the judge continued. "With scores of 196 points we have Gregory Martin and his German shepherd, Toronto's Mighty Merlin." The judge paused, allowing the crowd to clap again. "And then we have Kyla Hanton and her pug, Black Petunia Lass."

Kyla sucked her breath in so fast she almost choked. They had won a ribbon! A first-place ribbon! With a score of 196 out of 200 points!

Petunia pranced by Kyla's leg as they went forward to accept the beautiful rosette. The judge shook Kyla's hand firmly and then leaned over to speak quietly to her for a moment.

"That was a wonderful job, Dear," the judge said. "I have never seen a pug perform so well in obedience. You both must have worked very hard."

"We did," Kyla admitted.

There was a flash of light as her mother took her photo, and the crowd clapped one more time. Kyla left the ring, her ribbon in one hand, and Petunia's leash in the other. What a wonderful, wonderful day!

When Kyla was finally home that evening,

she hung the ribbon over her bed and then lay down to look at it.

I can't believe we did it, Kyla thought happily. *It seems like a dream.*

Kyla closed her eyes. *Dear Jesus,* she prayed quietly. *Thank You for helping Petunia and me do so well today. Thank You for helping Petunia become a good dog.* Kyla thought for another moment. *And even more, God, thank You for helping me become a good dog owner. I'm so glad You love me and forgive me when things go wrong. Please keep working with Petunia and me, because we both have lots of things to learn, amen.*

AUTHOR'S FOOTNOTE

The real Petunia's name was Dark Crystal. She started off sick and ugly and spoiled—and ended up a wonderful dog. She won her CD and her CDX title in obedience and had several champion puppies. She was the perfect family dog and never bit anyone in her entire life. She died at the age of thirteen, and I still miss her a lot.

I hope you remember that Jesus has a plan for your life. He loves you even when you are not perfect. And He'll help you to become better. All you need to do is trust and follow Him.

Heather Grovet

If you enjoyed this book, you'll enjoy these other books in the **Julius and Friends series**:

Julius, the Perfectly Pesky Pet Parrot
VeraLee Wiggins.
0-8163-1173-0. US$6.99, Cdn$10.99.

Julius Again!
VeraLee Wiggins.
0-8163-1239-7. US$6.99, Cdn$10.99.

Tina, the Really Rascally Red Fox
VeraLee Wiggins.
0-8163-1321-0. US$6.99, Cdn$10.99.

Skeeter, the Wildly Wacky Raccoon
VeraLee Wiggins.
0-8163-1388-1. US$6.99, Cdn$10.99.

Lucy, the Curiously Comical Cow
Corinne Vanderwerff.
0-8163-1582-5. US$5.99, Cdn$9.49.

Thor the Thunder Cat
VeraLee Wiggins.
0-8163-1703-8. US$6.99, Cdn$10.99.

Prince, the Persnickety Pony
Heather Grovet.
0-8163-1787-9. US$6.99, Cdn$10.99.

Prince Prances Again
Heather Grovet.
0-8163-1807-7. US$6.99, Cdn$10.99.

Order from your ABC by calling **1-800-765-6955**, or get online and shop our virtual store at **www.adventistbookcenter.com**.
• Read a chapter from your favorite book
• Order online
• Sign up for email notices on new products